Samuel French Acting Edition

Future Thinking

by Eliza Clark

SAMUELFRENCH.COM   SAMUELFRENCH.CO.UK

FOR PRODUCTION ENQUIRIES

UNITED STATES AND CANADA
Info@SamuelFrench.com
1-866-598-8449

UNITED KINGDOM AND EUROPE
Plays@SamuelFrench.co.uk
020-7255-4302

Each title is subject to availability from Samuel French, depending upon country of performance. Please be aware that *FUTURE THINKING* may not be licensed by Samuel French in your territory. Professional and amateur producers should contact the nearest Samuel French office or licensing partner to verify availability.

MUSIC USE NOTE

Licensees are solely responsible for obtaining formal written permission from copyright owners to use copyrighted music in the performance of this play and are strongly cautioned to do so. If no such permission is obtained by the licensee, then the licensee must use only original music that the licensee owns and controls. Licensees are solely responsible and liable for all music clearances and shall indemnify the copyright owners of the play(s) and their licensing agent, Samuel French, against any costs, expenses, losses and liabilities arising from the use of music by licensees. Please contact the appropriate music licensing authority in your territory for the rights to any incidental music.

IMPORTANT BILLING AND CREDIT REQUIREMENTS

If you have obtained performance rights to this title, please refer to your licensing agreement for important billing and credit requirements.

FUTURE THINKING was commissioned and first produced by South Coast Repertory with support from the Elizabeth George Foundation in Costa Mesa on April 1, 2016. The performance was directed by Lila Neugebauer, with sets by Dane Laffrey, costumes by Melissa Trn, lights by Lap Chi Chu, and sound by Stowe Nelson. The Production Stage Manager was Kathryn Davies and the Dramaturg was Kimberly Colburn. The cast was as follows:

PETER FORD . . . . .Arye Gross

JIM BARNARD. . . . . Enver Gjokaj

CHIARA FARROW. . . . . Virginia Vale

CRYSTAL FARROW. . . . . .Heidi Dippold

SANDY MILLS . . . . .Jud Williford

CHARACTERS

PETER FORD – a super fan, fifties, male

JIM BARNARD – a security guard, late thirties, male

CHIARA FARROW – a superstar, twenty-three, female

CRYSTAL FARROW – a stage mom, late forties, female

SANDY MILLS – a bodyguard, early forties, male

SETTING

Three hotels rooms in San Diego, CA

TIME

The Present

Scene One

*(**PETER FORD** sits in a hotel room. The room is under construction and has been converted into a kind of makeshift holding area for the security personnel of a large comic book/TV/movie convention. **PETER** is wearing a costume – a very tight spandex number with an elaborate, homemade design. He is dressed as "Gregor," a character in the fictional universe of a TV show called* Odyssey.*)*

*(**JIM BARNARD**, a security officer, enters the room.)*

JIM. I like your get-up.

*(**PETER** looks at him, feebly.)*

It's the guy from *Odyssey*, right?

PETER. Gregor.

JIM. My favorite's the one guy with the arm. The robot arm. What's his name?

PETER. Arthur 3-1-7.

JIM. Arthur 3-1-7.

(Suddenly grave.)

Peter, do you know why you're here?

Typically, we don't like to remove anyone from the con. You paid good money for those tickets and I'm sure you waited in line and we don't like to ruin anyone's fun, you understand. That's what this is supposed to be about, fun, and we don't like to ruin it for anyone.

PETER. I understand.

JIM. However, if there are legal documents there's not a lot we can do, is there?

(Beat.)

JIM. You knew she would be at that booth, didn't you?

PETER. No.

JIM. The sole purpose of the booth was to meet Chiara. That was the whole point of the booth, that's how it was advertised.

PETER. I didn't mean to... I was on my way to the...

JIM. You don't look like a dangerous person.

PETER. I'm not.

JIM. You seem like a nice guy.

PETER. Yes. I am.

JIM. I'm sure you are. But my hands are tied. She has a restraining order against you and you're in violation of that restraining order when you go to a booth where she's signing autographs, y'understand that?

PETER. Sure but –

JIM. I can't let you back out on the floor, now.

PETER. But, no, these tickets, I spent –

JIM. I understand that you did. Heck, I told my own kids we couldn't afford it this year. But Peter, you're in violation.

PETER. I didn't know it was her booth.

JIM. Well, honestly, I'm not sure you should have come here at all. I think that's asking for a situation, don't you think?

> *(Beat.)*

Were you asking for a situation?

PETER. No.

JIM. She's a twenty-three-year-old girl.

PETER. I'm not dangerous.

JIM. I know that. I know.

PETER. I like the show, that's all.

JIM. I'm sure that's true.

PETER. I like her show, I think she's a great performer, that's all. The guy, her bodyguard, he misunderstood me.

JIM. I'm sure that's true.

PETER. Last year, it was a misunderstanding.

JIM. You gave her a vial of your blood.

PETER. No.

JIM. That's what her guy said. He said last year you gave her a vial of your blood.

PETER. It wasn't my blood.

JIM. It was someone else's blood?

PETER. No. Well, no, it was mine, but –

JIM. Do you see how that's a problem, Peter?

PETER. On the show, it's how you –

>   *(Starting over.)*

In a world where money doesn't exist and diseases have overrun the colony, clean blood is the only currency –

JIM. In this world, giving someone a vial of your blood is a little strange, don't you think? It's bizarre, Peter, sorta deranged is what it is.

PETER. But she's on the show, she understands the reference –

JIM. This year you proposed to her.

PETER. That's not what happened.

JIM. You don't know her, Peter. You like her character but you don't know the girl.

PETER. I know that.

JIM. Do you mind me asking how old you are?

PETER. I'm fifty-one.

JIM. You're fifty-one, and how old is she?

PETER. Twenty-three.

JIM. That's almost thirty years. I know that happens in Hollywood sometimes, but not in the real world. It shouldn't happen in the real world. She's a kid. Do you have kids?

PETER. Yes.

JIM. Are they here with you at the con?

PETER. No.

JIM. How many kids? How old?

PETER. Ten and thirteen.

JIM. Girls? Boys?

PETER. The ten-year-old's a boy, thirteen-year-old's a girl.

JIM. Okay, so thirteen, that's ten years away from being twenty-three. You blink your eyes, your daughter'll be twenty-three. How would you like it if some guy, some fifty-one-year-old –

PETER. But that's not what's happening here –

JIM. There are plenty of older actresses you could admire. I like that Heather Locklear, you know her?

PETER. I know who she is.

JIM. She's a hottie, right?

PETER. Sure, she's attractive…

JIM. What about Heather Locklear?

PETER. I don't watch any of her shows.

JIM. Maybe you should. She's a regulation hottie.

PETER. You've seen *Odyssey*?

JIM. Once or twice, sure. My kid likes it.

(A beat as **PETER** *internalizes this insult.)*

PETER. Can I go now?

JIM. Go where?

PETER. Can I leave?

JIM. Well, I can't let you leave until I know whether she's pressing charges.

PETER. You're not a police officer, you can't hold me.

JIM. Well, actually we can, your ticket is a contract and when you come into the hall, you give us the right to keep everyone safe in the manner we see fit, it's a contract.

PETER. This is a hotel room.

JIM. This is "The Annex," that's what we call it. We've got over a hundred and thirty thousand patrons of this convention, hundreds of security personnel. Our offices are pretty busy this time of year, as I'm sure you can imagine. So this is The Annex. I petitioned for it, won. Here we are.

(*Okay then. A beat.*)

PETER. I'm supposed to call my kids, say good night.

JIM. It's the middle of the afternoon, Peter.

PETER. They're in Florida.

JIM. You came all the way from Florida?

PETER. They live in Florida.

JIM. Ohhh. Okay. I get it. This is a divorce situation.

PETER. I don't really think that's any of your business.

JIM. Of course not, Peter, I'm just making conversation.

PETER. Do I need a lawyer?

JIM. Why would you need a lawyer? I'm not a police officer.

(*Beat.*)

I'm trying to help you out here, that's why I mention Heather Locklear. I understand you like the show and I get that it's an important part of people's lives, these shows. I've been working the con ten years, okay? I understand about being a fan, heck, I enjoyed that new *Star Wars* just as much as the next guy, even waited in line to see those prequels, I didn't even think they were as bad as everyone said, okay? I liked a few parts in them, that's how much I like *Star Wars*. And I appreciated when they released the old ones all cleaned up, made better, with the CGI and all that.

PETER. That's not – that's not –

JIM. That's not what?

PETER. The CGI is terrible, it's a travesty, okay? It's a, a war crime.

(*Beat.*)

JIM. Who are you to tell me what it means to be a fan, Peter? You don't get to say who's a fan and who's not a fan, do you?

PETER. No.

JIM. No, that's right, no. I like the *Star Wars* films, you like this show *Odyssey*, and honestly, Peter, I'm okay with you liking a twenty-three-year-old hottie. I'm okay with it, I seen the show, she's a beautiful girl. I got no problem with what you do on your own time, I'm a man, I understand that. You're at home, you're alone, you're watching the show, whatever whatever, but, Peter –

PETER. That's not what it's about for me –

JIM. *But*, Peter, on the show this girl plays a soldier, she's a soldier?

PETER. Sort of.

JIM. She's a sort of soldier, she's a strong, hardened soldier type, but in real life, she's a girl, you understand? Maybe in the world of *Odyssey*, it's okay you like a girl soldier, so she's seen a lot of hardship and wars and whatnot and that makes her more mature. But in real life, this girl didn't graduate high school. She was on that other show before this one, that sitcom. She's a child actor. She grew up in Tarzana. This kid is a kid, Peter, and it's creepy to have some older gentleman at a comic book convention coming up to her asking her to marry him.

PETER. That's not what I was doing.

JIM. I've been working the con almost ten years, next year it'll be ten, and I see guys like you all the time, guys who have trouble telling the difference between the show and the real world. The problem comes when you start thinking you're part of that universe, like the universe of the show. Because when it all comes down to it, you're just a set of eyeballs for some bigwig Hollywood types, you understand that?

You're a set of eyeballs and a wallet and they hope you buy the lunch box and the box set and whatever else. They're banking on you liking this actress and wanting to buy the magazine where she shows her breasts or whatever.

PETER. That's a very cynical outlook.

JIM. I been working the con ten years.

PETER. I disagree with you. I strongly disagree with you.

JIM. Well, that's your right, Peter, I'm just sharing my insider knowledge from dealing with these bigwig Hollywood types. I run security for them, these bigwigs and they don't give a damn about the people here. They come for their parties and their booze and their cocaine and they don't give two shits about the people here.

PETER. You don't know anything about it.

JIM. Excuse me?

PETER. I'm just saying, with all due respect, I strongly disagree.

JIM. What do you do for work?

PETER. I'm a photographer.

JIM. See that's interesting.

PETER. Why?

JIM. What kinds of pictures you take?

PETER. I take pictures of people's pets.

JIM. Pets?

PETER. Yeah.

JIM. That's an industry?

PETER. I have a shop in the mall.

JIM. I see.

PETER. We take pictures of babies too.

JIM. I see.

PETER. People bring their babies in or their dogs, cats, rabbits sometimes, sometimes lizards, and there are costumes and they dress them up and then I take a picture, for a Christmas card or something like that. Portraits.

JIM. You enjoy that work?

PETER. Sure.

JIM. You always liked photography, when you were a kid?

PETER. Yeah, I guess so.

JIM. Like me, I always wanted to be a cop, I was a cop for Halloween every year. I made a little cardboard gun. It's my passion. That's how I got into security, it's a stepping stone. I'm applying for the academy in the fall.

PETER. Okay.

JIM. That's how it is for you? You're taking these pictures as a stepping stone? You wanna be a wildlife photographer or was this always your dream, taking pictures of people's pets.

PETER. I don't really think about it. It's a job.

JIM. I think it's important to have future goals. Keeps you moving forward. Like for me, when I become a cop, then I'm gonna want to be a lieutenant, and then after that I'm gonna want to be a detective, like a homicide detective, and then after my big career case, then I'm gonna be a sergeant, one of those politicos, you know, then I'm looking toward retirement, getting a boat, sailing around the world, see? Those are reasonable steps toward a reasonable goal. But you, you think you're gonna marry some twenty-three-year-old tarted up kid actress.

    (Beat.)

You had a ring in the bag, Peter.

PETER. You went through my belongings?

JIM. I had to sweep your materials for explosives.

PETER. Explosives?!

JIM. Your ticket is a contract, Peter. You sign the contract when you enter the hall.

PETER. This is a violation of my rights. I'm not just gonna sit here and let you enact your bizarre cop fantasies.

JIM. Maybe I should remind you that I'm the head of security for a convention that services over a hundred and thirty thousand people.

PETER. I understand and respect your importance.

JIM. You understand and respect my importance?

PETER. Yes.

JIM. That's rich. Oh boy, that's rich.

PETER. I'm not trying to disrespect you –

JIM. Let me give you a tip then, quit disrespecting me.

PETER. I'm sorry.

JIM. You don't want to be a wildlife photographer?

PETER. No.

JIM. Seems interesting to me. Going around the jungle, taking pictures of tribal people and panthers and whatnot. *National Geographic* type stuff.

PETER. It's not realistic for me to think I can be a wildlife photographer.

JIM. Why's that?

PETER. I don't have the training.

JIM. You take pictures of animals every day.

PETER. Domestic animals.

JIM. Lizards!

PETER. Iguanas, little tree lizards. Not, you know, not some big – I don't have the connections for that type of work.

JIM. Well, that's defeatist thinking.

PETER. I don't want to be a wildlife photographer.

JIM. I'm trying to help you, Peter.

PETER. Well just stop, please. If you don't mind, I'd like to see my ticket. I'd like to read this contract.

JIM. I'm your advocate here. I'm the one who could maybe talk to Chiara's security people and say, "Hey, get these charges dropped." But I'm also the guy who could say, "You know what? I think this dude is one sick motherfucker, he's a danger to himself and others. I think he should be banned from the con for life."

*(Silence from **PETER**.)*

You wouldn't want that, would you?

PETER. No sir.

JIM. No sir. That's exactly right.

> *(Beat.)*

That's exactly right.

> *(Lights.)*

Scene Two

(A hotel room. **CHIARA** *lies on the bed. Her mother,* **CRYSTAL***, wearing a pair of tight jeggings, sits flipping through her iPhone.* **CHIARA***'s bodyguard,* **SANDY***, stands by the door.)*

CHIARA. I'm so hungry.

CRYSTAL. What do you want?

CHIARA. Pudding.

CRYSTAL. Honey.

CHIARA. Can't we call someone? I want banana pudding.

CRYSTAL. Listen to this – banana pudding – don't be ridiculous.

CHIARA. Sandy?

CRYSTAL. Don't look at him. He's not your pudding butler, Chiara.

SANDY. Sorry, kiddo.

CHIARA. Mom, go back to your room.

CRYSTAL. I'm charging my phone.

CHIARA. There are plugs in your room.

CRYSTAL. I'm not leaving you after that craziness.

CHIARA. Mom, I'm a grown-ass woman.

CRYSTAL. The show needs to give you more protection at these things. Sandy needs to sleep, he can't be with you twenty-four hours a day.

SANDY. We handled the situation, Crys.

CRYSTAL. There's some lunatic running around thinking Chiara's his zombie bride or something. I'm not letting my daughter get stabbed by some weirdo…

SANDY. He didn't have a weapon.

CRYSTAL. Well, it's not just him, Sandy, it's all these weirdos.

CHIARA. They're not weirdos, Mom, they're my fans.

CRYSTAL. Listen to her – "my fans." Aren't you the little diva?

CHIARA. They just want to meet me.

CRYSTAL. I'm calling Danielle.

CHIARA. Go in the hall.

CRYSTAL. Excuse you.

CHIARA. I have a headache. Go in the hall if you're calling her.

> (CRYSTAL *begrudgingly stands and exits into the hall.* CHIARA *looks at* SANDY.)

I hate her.

SANDY. You don't hate her.

CHIARA. Sandy, you fucking hate her.

SANDY. Go easy on her, she's just trying to protect you.

CHIARA. I pay you to protect me. She just comes to these things so she can go to parties. She's wearing fucking jeggings! It's a horror show.

SANDY. You're her little girl. She likes being with you.

CHIARA. She likes being near me. It's not the same thing.

> (Beat.)

That guy…he's the blood guy from last year?

SANDY. We took care of it.

CHIARA. Does he really want to marry me?

SANDY. I don't know.

CHIARA. Maybe I should marry him, that would piss her off.

SANDY. That's not funny. He violated the restraining order.

CHIARA. He just likes taking pictures of me.

SANDY. You gotta start taking this stuff seriously.

> (Beat.)

CHIARA. If I give you five hundred bucks will you take my mom out for dinner?

SANDY. Stop it.

CHIARA. Please?! I want to go to this party and she's driving me crazy and I'm not bringing her. Let me direct your attention to Exhibit Jeggings.

SANDY. I should come with you.

CHIARA. Nobody takes security to these parties.

SANDY. There was a direct threat –

CHIARA. I'm not bringing a bodyguard to Jayden's room. I'll look like a brat, like I think I'm Beyoncé or something. Do me a solid and get Crystal drunk.

SANDY. No.

CHIARA. Believe me, I wouldn't want to either, that's why I'll pay you.

SANDY. Chiara.

CHIARA. Dude. You're taking my mom to the bar, you're getting her sloppy, she's definitely going to put her hands on you, you can make a decision from there, I'm not judging, do what you want, you're a single man, but she's not coming to this party with me and neither are you. Mmkay?

SANDY. You should be nicer to her, she does a lot for you.

CHIARA. And she'll do a lot for you too, Sandy, if you let her.

SANDY. Come on.

CHIARA. You never laugh.

SANDY. I laugh.

CHIARA. I've never seen you laugh.

SANDY. I need to be alert.

(**CHIARA** *flips through a magazine.*)

CHIARA. Did you see this picture of me in *US Weekly*?

SANDY. No.

CHIARA. Yes you did.

SANDY. I don't read those things.

CHIARA. You're such a liar. You totally read them. I look hot. Don't I look hot?

(*She shows him the magazine.*)

SANDY. It's a nice photo.

CHIARA. What is wrong with you?

SANDY. What should I say?

CHIARA. Say what you're thinking, dude. I look fucking hot in that picture. I bet you never masturbate.

SANDY. Chiara.

CHIARA. The first time I masturbated it was with this vibrating Mr. Potato Head and it was fucking magnificent. I wasn't even alive until that sexy vibrating potato.

SANDY. You're trying to get a rise out of me.

CHIARA. *(Re: a page in the magazine.)* Ugh, Jennifer Lawrence, shut up.

> (**CHIARA** *eyes* **SANDY**, *noticing he is not really listening to her.*)

You're in a hotel filled with people who are down to bone, you should go out and get some.

SANDY. I'm working.

CHIARA. Well, not tonight you're not, tonight you're getting Crystal drunk and I'm sorry for you but also maybe I'm not, maybe I'm also a little excited for you, because I'm pretty sure you're celibate and that's no way to live.

SANDY. You're lucky you don't have to have a real job.

CHIARA. Whoa! Tell me more about what a bad girl I am.

SANDY. Chiara.

CHIARA. No, I'm really naughty. I'm a bad, bad girl.

SANDY. These are the kinds of things you can't say in an office environment. It's sexual harassment.

CHIARA. Do you know how many people down there would pay money for me to sexually harass them?

SANDY. It's food for thought.

CHIARA. I don't want food for thought, I want banana pudding.

> (**CRYSTAL** *re-enters the room.*)

CRYSTAL. Danielle thinks we should press charges.

CHIARA. Fuck Danielle.

CRYSTAL. Chiara, stop it, I've had it up to here with you.

CHIARA. I'm not a fucking baby. Everyone leave my room!

>*(Throughout the following, **CRYSTAL** and **SANDY** ignore **CHIARA** and speak to each other.)*

CRYSTAL. Sandy, what do you think? You think this guy's dangerous?

SANDY.	**CHIARA**.
Well he was warned last year and he violated the restraining order –	I'm standing right here! I'm a person and I'm standing right here!

CRYSTAL.	
I just wish we could handle it quietly…	Oh my God, I'm fucking invisible.

SANDY.	
The restraining order's obviously a joke –	I could do anything right now.

CRYSTAL.	
It's just not…he's an older man, it's… y'know…	I could take a shit on this bed and no one would care.

SANDY.	
We'll be discreet, but we can't ignore it. He isn't going away…	I'M A GODDAMN TEA-POT SHORT AND TAKING A SHIT ON THIS BED!

>*(Beat.)*

CRYSTAL. *(Turning to **CHIARA**.)* Do you need attention? It seems like you really need attention right now.

CHIARA. This is my room! This is my room and I'm inviting you both to Get. The. Fuck. Out!

CRYSTAL. You're throwing a tantrum in front of Sandy.

CHIARA. I'm always in front of Sandy. My life is a one-woman show and Sandy is the only fucking audience member.

CRYSTAL. Ignore her. She's tired.

CHIARA. You're right. I am tired. Because I've been working all day and you've been sitting around on your jeggings butt making slutty faces at dudes in spandex.

CRYSTAL. CHIARA!

(**CHIARA** *sits on the bed in a pouty heap.*)

CHIARA. I'm a prisoner in my own life.

SANDY. Maybe we should let her take a nap.

CHIARA. Oh my God, *let* me take a nap?! I'm not a dog!

SANDY. I'm just saying, give you some privacy.

CRYSTAL. Security is waiting on word from us about what to do with this guy.

CHIARA. Does anyone want to ask me? Do I get a say in any of this?

CRYSTAL. Sure, Chiara, what do you think we should do?

CHIARA. I think we should release him, invite him up to your room and tell him that you are ready for a good time.

CRYSTAL. You're terrible, you know that? You're very cruel.

CHIARA. Do I need to Macaulay Culkin your jeggings ass?

CRYSTAL. Please. Please do. That would be terrific. Then maybe I could go back to having a life of my own.

CHIARA. Oh my GOD, by all means, PLEASE! PLEASE GO BACK TO HAVING A LIFE OF YOUR OWN.

SANDY. Ladies, I'm going to go take a shower.

CRYSTAL. Ugh, I'm sorry, Sandy. I'm so sorry.

SANDY. I just need about a half hour, and then I'll meet you back here? We can walk you to dinner, Chiara?

CHIARA. I'm not going to dinner. I'm staying here. You're going to dinner. The two of you.

CRYSTAL. We're not leaving you alone.

CHIARA. You are leaving me alone, because I said you're leaving me alone and I pay both your salaries. You and Sandy are going to go to dinner and have a great time, on me, and I'm going to go to Jayden's room SANS YOU.

CRYSTAL. Fine. Okay, fine. If that's what she wants, that's what she gets. Sandy, is that okay with you? Dinner in a half hour? A little break from the monster?

> (**SANDY** *looks at* **CHIARA**. *She smiles like a little evil troll.*)

SANDY. That sounds great.

CHIARA. This is the greatest day of my life.

> (**SANDY** *exits the room.* **CRYSTAL** *shoots* **CHIARA** *a look.*)

What?

CRYSTAL. You better hope he doesn't sell his story to a magazine.

CHIARA. What story?

CRYSTAL. The story of what a little twat you're being.

CHIARA. Oh my God, you just called me a twat?!

> (**CHIARA** *flops down on the bed and opens the magazine again.*)

CRYSTAL. Are you gonna shower?

CHIARA. No.

CRYSTAL. Don't you think you should shower?

CHIARA. No.

CRYSTAL. Honey, what about…

CHIARA. YOU TAKE A SHOWER.

CRYSTAL. I'm going to.

CHIARA. Good. Wash your hair.

> (**CRYSTAL** *moves to the bathroom door.*)

Not here! You have a room!

CRYSTAL. I was getting a hairbrush. Geez Louise.

CHIARA. Mom. I'm exhausted. I have early-onset carpal tunnel from signing all day…

CRYSTAL. You want some Advil?

CHIARA. No.

CRYSTAL. It's an anti-inflammatory…

CHIARA. Mom.

CRYSTAL. Fine. You don't want my help.

> (**CRYSTAL** *grabs a hairbrush from the bathroom.*
> *She moves back into the hotel room, brushing her*
> *hair.* **CHIARA** *flips the pages of her magazine.*)

Did you see your picture?

CHIARA. Yeah.

CRYSTAL. You look good.

CHIARA. I look fucking great.

CRYSTAL. Brett'll be happy. See? All that hard work…

CHIARA. They shouldn't have cropped you out. Your hair looked really good. I'm glad you did the highlights.

CRYSTAL. Me too.

> (**CRYSTAL** *moves to* **CHIARA**, *sitting next to her on*
> *the bed.*)

I wish they would leave you alone.

CHIARA. No you don't.

CRYSTAL. Of course I do. You could get in a car accident. That one guy on the bike… I mean, he barely knows how to ride that thing. His camera's like fifty pounds. What if he fell off and you ran him over?

CHIARA. Then maybe he'd back off.

CRYSTAL. I just wish they'd be more careful. It's scary.

CHIARA. I'm not scared of them.

> (**CRYSTAL** *starts brushing* **CHIARA***'s hair.* **CHIARA**
> *lets her. They don't talk about it. The hair brushing*
> *continues as…*)

CRYSTAL. Donna told me you gave them the finger yesterday.

CHIARA. Fuck Donna.

CRYSTAL. Chiara.

CHIARA. There were like eight guys in my face with cameras. They were in the way of this little girl who wanted an autograph. She was like seven. I told them to move and they wouldn't…

CRYSTAL. They'll print a story about that…

CHIARA. Who gives a shit?

CRYSTAL. Danielle does.

CHIARA. Fuck Danielle.

CRYSTAL. You know, if you give them a smile, let them take the picture they might leave you alone.

CHIARA. No they won't.

CRYSTAL. Well you shouldn't curse at them. What if they got video? That never goes away.

*(Suddenly **CHIARA** notices that **CRYSTAL** is brushing her hair.)*

CHIARA. What are you doing? Stop it.

CRYSTAL. I was just…

CHIARA. I'm taking a shower. Stop it.

*(**CHIARA** gets up and walks toward the bathroom.)*

Go back to your room.

*(**CHIARA** enters the bathroom, shuts the door. **CRYSTAL** sits alone on the bed.)*

(Lights.)

Scene Three

(Back in The Annex, **PETER** *and* **JIM** *are at a stand-off.)*

PETER. I think I should call a lawyer.

JIM. Oh yeah? You got a lawyer?

PETER. My sister's a lawyer.

JIM. By all means, call your sister. I'm sure she'd love to hear about the vials of blood you've been handing out like Halloween candy.

PETER. How much longer do you expect I'll be here?

JIM. They're discussing a plan of action. They are determining whether or not they will press charges. And then, of course, it's up to me to decide whether or not you'll be allowed to return to the convention in future years.

  (Beat.)

PETER. How am I supposed to know you're "Head of Security"? Your lanyard?

JIM. I'm Head of Security. Don't worry about it.

  (Beat.)

What do you see in this girl anyway?

  (No response.)

You bought her a ring. It was a nice ring, too, fancy. Musta really cost you.

PETER. You wouldn't understand.

JIM. I've been married eight years, my friend. I understand plenty.

PETER. I wasn't proposing to her.

JIM. Okay. It was a ring, though.

PETER. It was a gesture of sacrifice.

JIM. Like some Indian thing?

PETER. No.

  (Taking a deep breath.)

In *Odyssey*, there's this tribunal, it's made up of warlords basically, dictators, it's all the rich guys in the colony who disrupted the constitutional system when Earth was destroyed – you're not even listening.

JIM. Yes I am.

PETER. Forget it.

JIM. You're here. I'm here. We can sit here in silence, you can be a crankle-puss, or we can talk, those are your choices.

 (Beat.)

PETER. The tribunal, they're called the Unity Council…

PETER.	**JIM**.
…Took over when the president-elect was assassinated, and they've been rooting out soldiers loyal to the democracy and executing them publicly, and Sabrina, that's the character she plays, Sabrina's a kind of soldier, she's not on the official roster because she was too young to enlist, but she's a symbol for the resistance.	Okay, Unity Council.

PETER. …She killed Dimitri and he was one of the most ruthless of these guys, so she's been adopted by the cause and held up as a symbol for those people who still have hope.

JIM. I see.

PETER. She represents hope for the future of the colony. For democracy.

JIM. She's Obama on Mars.

 (A frustrated beat. Then:)

PETER. What's your favorite show?

JIM. My wife and I watch *The Voice*.

PETER. That's not a show.

JIM. Yes it is.

PETER. It's a reality competition. It's not a show.

JIM. Oh, I'm sorry, we turn on the TV and magically it's on. It's called *The Voice*.

(PETER, exasperated, moves on.)

PETER. Clean blood is the only currency in this world, because it can treat a bunch of the afflictions on the colony, and also it's a symbol –

JIM. Awful lot of symbols in this show.

PETER. It's a *symbol* of the family. Because only a hundred thousand people were able to escape from Earth before the fires, so now, forty years later, a lot of us are related. It's a gesture of goodwill, giving a vial of clean blood. It means, "We're family. All of us. And we will survive."

JIM. I didn't realize this show was so weird.

PETER. I was participating in the community of the show, the blood was a gesture, and the ring was a –

JIM. Symbol, yeah. Of family or outer space or something.

PETER. Don't you ever wish you were a part of something?

JIM. I am a part of something. I got kids, I got a wife, I'm part of the security staff here – the *head of it*, I belong to a church, Jesus what else? I got a bowling league…

PETER. And those things satisfy you?

JIM. Sure. What the hell?

PETER. You're lucky that you feel satisfied by those small things.

JIM. My church happens to be one of the largest churches in the area and I got six brothers and sisters so my family ain't too small either.

PETER. You want to be a cop, right? And then a detective and then you'll get a boat?

JIM. Yeah.

PETER. And you got kids right? And you want your kids to grow up and get good jobs and make lots of money and then buy their own boat.

JIM. They don't need a boat. They can use my boat.

PETER. Right. Fine. The point is, there's always that future thing, that striving, that one more thing you want, and that's what makes you a prisoner. You're working toward some happy ending, but there are no endings. The striving keeps you moving forward when there might be something sideways.

JIM. Sideways.

PETER. Time is circular, that's the thing that Sabrina discovers. It's like a drop of water, right? Like you put a drop of water in a cup and it spreads out in all directions, forwards, backwards, sideways, even up and down a little and then when it hits the edge of the cup, it comes back. It dissolves into the rest of the water, once you drop it in, it becomes a part of all the rest of the water, there's no fishing out that one droplet ever again.

JIM. Well, this has been highly enlightening.

PETER. You're not listening.

JIM. Oh boy, I'm listening, alright, I hear you loud and clear. All you fanboys like to talk about is time travel, time is circular and whatever else. It's fascinating stuff, Peter, I've done my fair share of thinking about it, believe me, I have. My neighbor and I wrote a screenplay on the subject, okay? But I'm asking you why you would give a vial of blood to a kid actress and you still can't manage to give me a satisfactory answer to that one, which makes me think you haven't learned your lesson, which makes me think we ought to ban you from the convention for life.

(Beat. **PETER** *considers this.)*

PETER. She seems like she understands.

JIM. She doesn't understand geography much less the space-time continuum. For Christ's sakes, Peter, she's a pair of tits.

PETER. Don't say that.

JIM. I'll say what I want, it's my Annex.

PETER. That's, that's, uh, she's not a, she's not what you said she is, and it's offensive, it's offensive you would say that.

JIM. Right, Peter, 'cause she's a warrior. You need to learn to separate the actress from the character. The show's not real, okay?

PETER. I know that. I know.

JIM. What happened to your kids, Peter?

> *(No response.)*

Your wife took them away? Because she didn't like this nonsense with the actress?

PETER. She didn't understand.

JIM. Well of course she didn't, she's a woman, she's your wife and you're obsessed with some girl.

PETER. That's not how it is.

JIM. Where do you live? Where's the pet photography shop?

PETER. Ohio.

JIM. That's a long way from Florida. When's the last time you saw your kids, Peter?

PETER. Christmas.

JIM. That was seven months ago.

PETER. She doesn't like to come to Ohio and she doesn't want the kids traveling alone.

JIM. Don't you have any rights?

PETER. I don't want to upset them.

JIM. Don't you think it upsets them not to see their father?

PETER. I don't know.

JIM. Don't you think they might like to come to one of these conventions? There's lots of great stuff for kids here, more oriented toward kids than grown-ups, frankly.

PETER. They don't watch television. She doesn't let them.

JIM. She doesn't let the kids watch TV?

PETER. No.

JIM. Well, that's a ridiculous rule, Peter. I don't mind telling you, since she's your ex, but that's a ridiculous rule.

PETER. I know.

JIM. When did she move to Florida?

PETER. Ten months ago.

JIM. And how long were you together before that?

PETER. Fifteen years.

JIM. And they were good, those years?

PETER. Yes.

JIM. You loved her?

PETER. Yes.

JIM. Why don't you go to Florida, Peter? Why don't you try and go be with your family? Enough of this actress nonsense. You need to learn to live in the present, like you said, like you were saying about the drop of water, you're the drop of water, Peter, and your family's the cup and you need to spread out in all directions, be with them. Your kids'll be grown before you know it.

PETER. The cup is time.

JIM. Okay okay so I messed up your cup thing, who cares? It was stupid, Peter, it's a stupid idea. Time starts when you're born and it stops when you die and in the meantime it moves forward one day at a time and you only got so many days on this earth and you ought to be with your kids.

(No response.)

You know I'm right.

PETER. She seems lonely.

JIM. Your wife?

PETER. No.

JIM. *(Realizing he means* **CHIARA**.*)* She seems lonely to you? It seems lonely to have millions of dollars and a mansion in Beverly Hills and eight million boyfriends and a *royce roils* or whatever else?

PETER. Yes.

JIM. You know who's lonely? You. You're the lonely one. Your wife kicked you out, you don't get to see your kids. That's lonely.

> *(Beat.)*

You ever see a shrink Peter?

PETER. Yes.

JIM. What does your shrink say?

PETER. What do you mean?

JIM. You get a diagnosis for all this?

PETER. I'm depressed.

JIM. You're depressed.

PETER. Yes.

JIM. Clinically.

PETER. Yes.

JIM. I think you might have a bit more going on in there, Peter.

> *(Lights.)*

Scene Four

(SANDY's hotel room. SANDY mixes a drink on the shitty hotel table. A toilet flushes, and CRYSTAL exits the bathroom.)

CRYSTAL. This place has great soap. Coconut mint something? Smell.

(CRYSTAL pushes her hands into SANDY's face. He takes them in his, pulls them close to his nose, inhales.)

Hi.

SANDY. Hi.

(SANDY relaxes into her arms – they kiss. A familiar kiss. This is clearly not the first time this has happened.)

Should we check on her?

CRYSTAL. Oh please, she wants us to go die somewhere, let her stew in it.

SANDY. I know she puts on that brave face, but it's gotta be a little scary for her.

CRYSTAL. She's loving every minute of it. Please.

(SANDY hands her the drink.)

Thank you Jesus.

SANDY. You didn't tell her about us.

CRYSTAL. It's none of her business either way, so no, I haven't told her, but so what if she finds out.

SANDY. I work for her, Crys.

CRYSTAL. Actually, no, you work for me.

SANDY. I got a headache.

CRYSTAL. You want me to rub your head?

SANDY. Nah, it's okay.

CRYSTAL. Siddown. C'mon. You sit down on the floor okay? Put your back up against me.

(**SANDY** *sits down on the floor.* **CRYSTAL** *sits on the edge of the bed. He releases his head into her hands and* **CRYSTAL** *massages his temples.*)

CRYSTAL. Relax.

(*A sharp command.*)

Relax.

SANDY. You don't have to –

CRYSTAL. Shhhhh.

(**SANDY** *relaxes as* **CRYSTAL** *massages his temples.*)

Next week she's back to work so set security can take care of her if you wanna go see your baby or…

SANDY. Yeah.

CRYSTAL. Bet she's getting big.

SANDY. Deb's mom sent me a video. She's gonna walk any day.

CRYSTAL. You'll wanna be there for that.

SANDY. Yeah.

CRYSTAL. You tell Deb about us?

SANDY. No.

CRYSTAL. Oh.

SANDY. I'm gonna. I'm gonna tell her, I just…

CRYSTAL. Nah, it's okay.

SANDY. I just don't want to jeopardize my visits with Amber.

CRYSTAL. Deb's not some saint. She's got her own guy now, she can't begrudge you.

SANDY. I know that.

CRYSTAL. Well, whatever you think.

SANDY. I just wanna do the right thing. For my kid.

CRYSTAL. Yeah.

(**SANDY** *gets up, walks toward the window. Outside, there's some kind of laser light show.*)

SANDY. What the hell are they doing out there?

(*Beat.*)

I was thinking, maybe you and Chiara need a break from each other, like a little vacation or something. I could take her back to set for a week or so if you wanna go take care of your own stuff?

CRYSTAL. What did she say to you?

SANDY. Nothing. She didn't say anything.

CRYSTAL. Bullshit.

SANDY. Honestly.

CRYSTAL. Is she serious about this divorce thing? She knows she can't divorce me, she's not even a minor.

SANDY. She didn't say anything to me.

CRYSTAL. You're not her dad.

SANDY. I know that.

CRYSTAL. She doesn't need a dad. She needs a kick in the ass. I'm supposed to apologize for wanting the best for my kid?

SANDY. Of course not.

CRYSTAL. I know you think I'm like a total shit parent, but I'm telling you, she was always like this, it's like an innate part of her personality. Like genetic. 'Cept she didn't get it from me. She's like that bald little freak in those *Hobbit* movies. That Gollum. You'll see, when Amber gets big, you can teach 'em but they don't learn it unless it's in 'em already.

SANDY. She's just a kid.

CRYSTAL. When I was twenty-three I was bussing tables in fucking Omaha, getting my ass cupped by the manager three times a day, washing dishes 'cause the guy wouldn't let me in the front 'less I'd let him fuck me, which I wouldn't cuz I was so goddamned worried what my ma would think.

SANDY. I wasn't saying –

CRYSTAL. So excuse me if I don't think that getting catered meals brought to your trailer in between set-ups is some kind of slave labor. You know I never went anywhere? Never anywhere outside of Nebraska 'til I was twenty-five. Didn't get a passport 'til Chiara did *Thrill Seekers 2* in Paris.

SANDY. She's still got pressures, expectations. I'm not saying it's the same, just that –

CRYSTAL. I'm telling you, one day she's this little kid, looking up at you with big blue eyes, listening to every word you say like there's magic in it, the next day she's…*that*…whatever she is.

SANDY. Crystal…

CRYSTAL. I know my kid, okay? You're giving me a headache.

SANDY. Sorry.

> *(A beat. But* **CRYSTAL** *isn't done.)*

CRYSTAL. Like I wouldn't like to sit down every once in awhile. Like I wouldn't like to just be in a place and have anyone care for one second if I'm hungry. You know, she wouldn't eat if I didn't remind her.

> *(Beat.)*

I liked it when she was a baby, you know?

SANDY. She's an adult now.

CRYSTAL. Oh yeah? You think so?

SANDY. She's twenty-three.

CRYSTAL. She knows how to remember names – she can tell you every single person who works in the casting department or all the hairdressers and what their kids are called and all about their boyfriends. But like, can she write a check? Does she know how to put gas in a car? She's never even been grocery shopping.

SANDY. She won't learn unless you let her.

> *(***CRYSTAL** *suddenly turns to* **SANDY**, *heated.)*

CRYSTAL. You have a nine-month-old so now you think you know what it's like to be a parent? You haven't seen your kid in six weeks, for fuck's sake.

> *(***SANDY** *looks at her, surprised, a little hurt. He gets up to mix himself another drink.)*

Sorry.

SANDY. It's fine.

CRYSTAL. Sand, I'm sorry.

SANDY. It's fine.

CRYSTAL. You're pissed now. You're mad at me.

SANDY. You're right. What do I know?

CRYSTAL. You know plenty. I'm terrible. C'mon, I created that monster, so it's in me too okay? I'm an asshole.

SANDY. No you're not.

CRYSTAL. We're the only two people keeping her from starving to death. She's hopeless without us.

> *(There is frantic knocking on **SANDY**'s hotel room door.)*

Who is that?

SANDY. I don't know.

CRYSTAL. You order something?

> *(**SANDY** approaches the door.)*

CHIARA. *(Offstage.)* SANDY!! OPEN THE FUCKING DOOR!

CRYSTAL. Fuck. Shit.

> *(**CHIARA** starts to wiggle the door handle and bang louder.)*

CHIARA. *(Offstage)* LET ME IN!! SANDY!

> *(**CRYSTAL** and **SANDY** scramble. **CRYSTAL** hides in the bathroom, shuts the door.)*

> *(**SANDY** opens the door. **CHIARA**, drunk, stumbles in.)*

Hey. What the fuck.

SANDY. I thought you were at the party.

CHIARA. The party? Sucked.

> *(**CHIARA** flops onto **SANDY**'s bed.)*

Can I have some? Thirsty.

> *(**CHIARA** points to **SANDY**'s drink.)*

SANDY. How much have you had already?

CHIARA. What're you, the police?

SANDY. You seem like you've had enough.

CHIARA. I'm of the legal age, man. I'm a grown-up, man.

> *(Off his look.)*

I had some champagne in Jayden's room, and I smoked some pot. Two puffs. Three puffs. I didn't even inhale. God.

SANDY. Why don't you have some water?

> *(He hands her a bottle of water. She starts to drink it, sucking it down. She spills it on her shirt.)*

CHIARA. Oops.

> *(**SANDY** takes the bottle from her, caps it.)*

Sorry. Your bed's wet. It's not pee. I swear.

SANDY. It's okay. Maybe I should take you back to your room, let you lie down?

CHIARA. Wanna watch a movie?

SANDY. I'm pretty tired.

CHIARA. C'mon like a short movie.

SANDY. Get up, kiddo. Bedtime.

> *(**CHIARA** flips off her high heels and crawls further onto **SANDY**'s bed, rooting herself into the pillows.)*

CHIARA. Your room's different than mine.

SANDY. Your room is nicer.

CHIARA. You have more pillows.

SANDY. They'll send more pillows if you ask them. You want me to call the desk?

CHIARA. Jayden was such a dick tonight. Like I was invisible. Like I was a ghost.

SANDY. You didn't talk to him?

CHIARA. I talked to him. For like a MINUTE. Then Jessa Andrews came in and everybody was like, "Oh my God, Jessa Andrews, sing that song and dance like a laser or whatever the fuck." And she did it. You believe that? She fucking did it. She has *one song*. One song. She doesn't even write her stuff. She doesn't play an instrument. She's not even good at dancing!

SANDY. It's just a novelty thing, 'cause she's got that song on the radio, I'm sure he likes you more…

CHIARA. Her song sucks. Jayden's like, "I love your song. It's so tiiiiiiiight." Like that, like he says it like that, all sexual. "It's so tiiiiiiiight." It's disgusting. He sounds like a rapist.

SANDY. For what it's worth, I never liked him for you. He always seemed like a punk.

CHIARA. You don't even *know* him!

(*Beat.*)

He seems like a punk?

SANDY. Yes.

CHIARA. He is a punk.

(*Beat.*)

But I feel like, I dunno, like maybe, like what if I love him, you know? Like what if he was my one chance at happiness and now he's with Jessa Andrews? They danced together. They like *choreographed* a routine. In front of everyone. Like a fucking talent show. There were *rappers* there. You don't invite people over to your hotel room to show them your choreographed dance routine, okay? You don't invite *rappers* to watch that shit.

SANDY. You want some more water?

CHIARA. He looked so happy. He was drunk, but he was also, like, happy, you know? Like he's looking at her and she's dancing and it's like they're the only people in the room. Like I'm invisible, like I'm a ghost and the rappers are ghosts and we're all just ghosts and they're dancing. Or they're the ghosts and they don't even care about us, because they're the only two ghosts in the room.

SANDY. Honey, drink this.

CHIARA. Don't call me honey. I'm not a kid.

(**SANDY** *hands her the water and she drinks.*)

SANDY. It's okay to be a kid.

CHIARA. Ew.

SANDY. I'm just saying, life gets very grown-up very fast and one day soon you'll wish you could go back.

CHIARA. I can't go back.

(*Beat.*)

Nobody's ever gonna love me like that.

SANDY. Of course they will. But you don't have to worry about that yet.

CHIARA. People my age have *babies*.

SANDY. They shouldn't.

CHIARA. Who's gonna have a baby with me?

SANDY. You shouldn't be thinking about having a baby.

CHIARA. Sometimes I think that's the only way to get my mom off my ass. Like if I had a baby then I'd be the mom, y'know?

SANDY. You need to sleep, okay? Let me take you back to your room.

CHIARA. I jus' tole you my whole life story, like practically crying my eyes out and you're tryin' to kick me out.

(*Beat.*)

You never see your kid. I know that's cuz of me.

SANDY. It's not because of you.

CHIARA. Yeah it is. I got ears. I know what Deb thinks of me.

SANDY. It was a mutual separation.

CHIARA. That's not a real thing.

SANDY. Sometimes it is, yes. Sometimes.

CHIARA. No, never. Like my mom and dad? Not mutual. My dad fucking left her ass. Ran off with some girl he worked with in the pharmacy. Like my age. They live in Hong Kong. She's from there.

SANDY. Well, sometimes –

CHIARA. Or me and Jayden. Not mutual. I fucking love him and he's ghost dancing with some pop skank in front of a room full of rappers right this minute.

> *(Beat.)*

Everybody loves somebody. But sometimes it doesn't work out. Like Deb thought you were a bad influence maybe, or maybe you hit her –

SANDY. I didn't hit her.

CHIARA. Or maybe you cheated on her or maybe nothing happened and she just stopped loving you or maybe she never loved you in the first place. That happens too. People just wind up together and then they wake up and they're like, "What the fuck am I doing?" And they leave. My dad did. Deb did. Everybody does. Or like the guy today, the guy who says he loves me. That guy's going to live the rest of his life and never get to be loved by the one person he loves. That's the saddest thing in the world.

SANDY. That man is ill, Chiara. He's delusional.

CHIARA. Says you. You haven't even talked to him.

> *(Beat.)*

I think we're the same. You and me. Maybe we're just unlovable.

SANDY. I have plenty of people who love me. So do you.

CHIARA. No. No we don't. Can I tell you a secret?

SANDY. Okay.

CHIARA. C'mere.

> (**SANDY** *tentatively creeps toward her.*)

SANDY. What is it?

CHIARA. If you want me, you can have me.

> (**SANDY**, *shocked, takes a step back.*)

SANDY. You need to go to sleep.

CHIARA. What?

SANDY. You're just, you're confused, honey, you're…

CHIARA. Don't call me that. Stop calling me that.

SANDY. Chiara.

CHIARA. I see the way you look at me. I know why Deb hates me and why she won't let you see your kid and I know about the fight you had in my trailer last year. I was just offering, 'cause you seem sad and lonely and so am I and I just thought…

SANDY. You have to go.

CHIARA. You know you want me. And I'm saying you can have me. You should be happy, Sandy.

SANDY. You need to go back to your room. C'mon.

> (*He starts gathering her shoes, trying to put them on her. She kicks them off.*)

CHIARA. Stop it. Stop it.

SANDY. C'mon. We'll talk in the morning, okay?

CHIARA. STOP IT.

> (**SANDY** *stops in his tracks.* **CHIARA** *starts to cry.*)

SANDY. C'mon, Chiara, don't…

> (*Beat.*)

Hey. Hey. You're very important to me, very important…

CHIARA. I can't even get *you* to love me.

> (**CHIARA** *stands up and walks toward the bathroom.* **SANDY** *stands paralyzed, unsure what to do.* **CHIARA** *tries the bathroom door. It's locked. She tries it again.*)

SANDY. C'mon, let's go back to your room, okay?

CHIARA. Why is it locked? Why is this door locked?

> (**CHIARA** *looks at* **SANDY**, *starting to comprehend what's happening, not wanting to.*)

COME OUT OF THERE!! COME OUT OF THERE!! COME OUT OF THERE!!

> (*She's having a temper tantrum. Tears streaming down her face, arms flailing against the door. And*

*then she steps away from the door as it slowly opens
and* **CRYSTAL** *comes out.)*

CRYSTAL. Honey.

*(***CHIARA*** looks at* **SANDY** *and then back at*
CRYSTAL. *She stops crying.)*

Baby, we've been meaning to talk to you, and there just
wasn't a right time, and...

*(***CHIARA*** looks at* **SANDY** *one last time and then
walks out of the room, leaving* **SANDY** *holding her
high heels.)*

(Lights.)

End of Act One

ACT TWO

Scene One

(JIM slowly savors some pathetic room service. PETER sits staring at him.)

(PETER's cell phone sits in the center of the table. Both men are fixated on the phone with intense focus.)

(Munch. Stare. Munch.)

(Finally the phone rings, piercing the silence. PETER and JIM both lunge for the phone. JIM gets it first, mouth full of french fry. He picks it up and holds it out in front of him until PETER slides back into his chair, defeated. Then, he hands PETER the phone.)

PETER. *(Into the phone.)* Hey, Annie? Yeah, hi. They gave you the message?

No, I don't know. Nothing. Nothing.

Of course not, of course…

No.

(JIM watches PETER intently, reacting to the things he's saying.)

He won't let me leave.

That's what I said.

There are no charges.

Well, I can't just walk out the door.

Because, I don't know, because he says…

No. No. I don't want to make trouble.

He's here. Right here.

(**JIM**, *amused, points at himself. Me?*)

(**PETER** *ignores him.*)

Like right here. Twenty feet.

No, it's a hotel room. He called it "The Annex."

NO!! You can't call her. No, Annie, please God, let's not, c'mon, no.

JIM. She wants to call the wife?

(**PETER** *ignores him.*)

PETER. *(Into the phone.)* I don't know, whatever you can.

I thought someone should at least know that I'm here. That I'm being held against my will.

JIM. That's dramatic. False and dramatic.

PETER. *(Into the phone.)* Nothing. He didn't say anything.

Forget it. I'm sorry I called.

Well I am. NO! Do not call her. Jesus, Annie, if you call her, I swear to fucking God...

JIM. Oh, Peter. Geez Louise.

PETER. *(Into the phone.)* He doesn't want to talk to you.

JIM. I'll talk to her.

PETER. *(Into the phone.)* Can't you just, like, can't you do something?

...He's saying my ticket is a contract...

JIM. It *is* a contract.

PETER. *(Into the phone.)* I didn't know it was her booth.

(*Suddenly solemn.*)

I know. I know what I said.

I'm sorry.

Please Annie...

(**PETER** *looks at* **JIM**. **JIM** *smiles and then extends his hand for the phone.* **PETER** *reluctantly hands it over.*)

(**JIM** *takes a deep, cleansing breath, then brings the phone to his ear.*)

JIM. Hello is this Annie?

This is James Barnard, Head of Security. You can call me Jim.

So you're a lawyer?

Where are you calling from?

Well, Aloha.

Annie, your brother's in a bit of trouble.

I'm not sure if he really "e-numerated" all the facts but you see there's a legal document called a restraining order. This document was filed last year when your brother brought a vial of blood to a young actress.

That means there's a precedent.

Now, Peter's saying this blood was, uh, some kind of offering, but as I'm sure you can imagine, blood is something we're not too keen on waving around here at the convention center.

No, you don't need to apologize for him.

I see.

Uh-huh, yeah, he mentioned that.

PETER. What is she saying?

JIM. *(Ignoring* **PETER**.*)* Well that's interesting.

I'm sure that's true.

Really? Wow.

He didn't mention that.

No, that's something we were unaware of.

PETER. What? What?

JIM. *(Into the phone.)* I'm sure. Yes, of course.

You get yourself a Mai Tai on me.

We're taking good care of him.

PETER.	**JIM**.
No. No you're not.	Okay.
(Toward the phone.)	Thanks so much.
No they're not! Annie!	Bye bye now.
You gotta help me!	

(**JIM** *hangs up the phone.* **PETER** *stares at him.*)

PETER. What did she say?

JIM. She said you're harmless.

PETER. And?

JIM. And you've gotten into this kind of trouble before.

PETER. No. No, she didn't say that.

JIM. She said you don't want her to call the wife, but she feels compelled...

PETER. No. No.

JIM. She feels that it's your wife's right to know what's going on. So she doesn't worry.

PETER. That's, that's, um, that's bullshit. I need to call her back. I need to...

JIM. Well, I told you not to call your sister but you don't take advice from guys with lanyards "enacting their cop fantasies" so...

PETER. So I'm fucking stuck here, in this goddamn back room bullshit with you, you *are BULLSHIT.*

JIM. I am bullshit?

PETER. Fuck!! Goddamn it! Shit cock!

JIM. You're gonna need to calm down, Peter. I'm gonna have to ask you to calm down.

> *(Beat.)*

"Shit cock"?

PETER. You've extradited me to some hotel room Guantanamo and now I'm here and you're not telling me what's happening and you could kill me!

JIM. Peter, you're getting overheated. Would you like a soda?

PETER. NO I WOULD NOT LIKE A SODA!!

> (**JIM** *screams at the top of his lungs. Beat.*)

JIM. Well. Now that we've cleared the air.

PETER. No. No. We have *not* cleared the air. Because you are sitting there with your smug bullshit face and I'm sitting here, your prisoner, and you think you've got me right where you want me and you can do whatever you want. You know what I think?

JIM. Of course not.

PETER. I think you are a very sad human being.

JIM. Do you now?

PETER. I do. I think you are a sad man with a sad sense of himself. Or no sense of himself. I think you wake up every day wishing that every single aspect of your little life was different. And then you come here and you're the king of your own little warped bullshit world and you mess with people like me because you can. That's what I think.

JIM. You're saying I'm like Biff. Like Biff from *Back to the Future.*

PETER. Fuck.

JIM. I got a sick kid you know.

> (**JIM** *shows* **PETER** *a picture on his phone.*)

Not the fat one. The other one. My daughter. She's just a baby, two years old. She's got bone cancer.

> (**PETER** *looks at* **JIM**, *not knowing what to say.*)

I don't expect you to say anything. I'm just telling you, things aren't always what you think they are. You might chew on that for a second.

PETER. I'm sorry.

JIM. Doctors say she's dying.

PETER. I'm sorry.

JIM. It's a shame. You know, obviously for us it's the tragedy of our lives, but for the world, you know? Because this kid's got something going on, something real special. 'Course I think that, right? She's my kid, but objectively, I'm saying she's got something special. Like, and this is just a little thing, but for months, we've been putting our trash out on the street for the truck and we come out in the morning and the cans are all fucked up, trash everywhere. I thought it was kids. Teenagers, or kids at my son's school teasing him because he's so fat. But then, last week, Stella, that's my daughter, she's doing this thing that she does sometimes, playing lighthouse. She sits on her bed and she points a flashlight out the window, flashes it around, like a lighthouse. Stupid. Anyways, she's flashing the light around and she points it at this tree, and there's four sets of eyes all lit up at the top of this really tall tree. Raccoons. That's who's been fucking up our trash cans. And I'm all pissed off, getting ready to take a chainsaw, cut the tree down, bash these fuckers' heads in with a baseball bat. You know, really take out some rage on these poor fucks. And Stella's like, "No Daddy." And then she points the flashlight up at the tree and she says, that one's the daddy, that one's the mommy, that one's the Ruben, that one's the Stella. They're a family, you know? Two years old, but she can see that.

> *(Beat.)*

Goddamn raccoons are gonna live longer than my kid.

> *(Beat.)*

PETER. Why are you telling me this?

JIM. You need a kick in the pants, Peter. You need a goddamn kick in the pants.

> *(The phone rings. JIM answers.)*

(Into the phone.) Jim Barnard, Head of Security.

Okay. Send him to The Annex.

Are you serious? It's Room 231!

> *(JIM hangs up the phone.)*

The bodyguard's on his way.

PETER. You gotta help me. You gotta help me, please.

JIM. And how exactly do you expect me to do that?

PETER. You gotta tell him I'm not dangerous.

JIM. Do I look like a psychologist?

PETER. I'm just a guy.

JIM. You know, maybe you need some help, man. I'm not saying this as James Barnard, Head of Security. I'm saying this as Jim, just one guy to another guy. You got a real tentative relationship with reality, man. And look at you. You don't go outside, I can tell that. That's just some deductive skills I'm using here. You get vitamins from the sun. Go outside! Go outside! Take a look around, throw a baseball with your kid, okay? Maybe turn the TV off. Get some perspective.

PETER. Please help me.

> *(There is a knock on the door.* **JIM** *opens it.* **SANDY** *is standing there.)*

SANDY. Hi, you're Jim?

JIM. Come on in. This is Peter.

> *(***SANDY** *enters the room.)*

Peter say hello.

PETER. I'm sorry about the confusion earlier.

JIM. *(To* **SANDY.***)* He's refusing to acknowledge that he knew he was in violation of the restraining order.

SANDY. *(To* **PETER.***)* Mr. Ford, I thought we had this conversation last year.

PETER. I'm sorry, sir. I really didn't know…

SANDY. It's my responsibility to protect Ms. Farrow.

PETER. I swear, I swear to God I didn't know.

SANDY. Mr. Ford, if you don't mind, I'm trying to explain something to you.

JIM. He's not respectful.

PETER. That's not, that's not true, sir.

JIM. Well, it is true.

PETER. Damn it, I'm just…

JIM. No need to cuss.

> *(To* **SANDY.***)*

See what I mean?

PETER. Let me start over. What can I call you? What's your name, sir?

SANDY. Sanford Mills.

PETER. Mr. Mills, please let me explain...

SANDY. I don't need an explanation. That's not really the point we're at now.

JIM. We're past that point.

SANDY. Hi, Jim, is it?

JIM. Yes, hi. Jim. Jim Barnard.

SANDY. Do you mind waiting outside?

JIM. Well, actually, yes I do mind. This is my Annex, first of all, and second of all, it's my responsibility to ensure the safety of the patrons of this convention.

SANDY. Okay. Fine, whatever.

> *(Moving on to* **PETER**.*)*

Mr. Ford, I've spoken to my client and it's our determination that there really is no other option but to press charges at this time.

PETER. No, I, sir, let me please...

JIM. This is kind of all he has.

SANDY. You'll be escorted from the convention center to the police station where you will be formally charged in violation of your restraining order.

PETER. What am I supposed to do now?

SANDY. We have to take this young woman's safety very seriously. As I'm sure you can understand.

PETER. I'm not a threat to her, I'm no threat...

JIM. He's been saying that for hours, but you know, Sanford, you mind if I call you Sanford? I think we're dealing with some mental illness issues...

SANDY. *(To* **JIM**.*)* Is there a place we might be able to talk?

JIM. You and me?

SANDY. Yes.

JIM. Sure thing. Sure thing.

> *(To* **PETER**.*)*

Bathroom break, Peter.

PETER. I don't need to use the bathroom.

JIM. You do need to use the bathroom, Peter, because this is a bathroom break.

> (**JIM** *opens the door to the bathroom.* **PETER** *looks to* **SANDY** *for a moment, sighs, then enters the bathroom.*)

> (**JIM** *looks to* **SANDY** – *"See what I did there?"* **SANDY** *doesn't react.*)

> (*Once the door to the bathroom is closed,* **SANDY** *smiles at* **JIM**.*)

SANDY. I can take it from here, Jim.

JIM. Great. I got your back.

SANDY. It's my responsibility to protect this young woman's life, do you understand that?

JIM. Of course I do.

SANDY. I need to scare the shit out of this guy, okay? You see he's back again this year, so the restraining order didn't do much good.

JIM. Yeah, yeah, I hear you. You just let me know what you want me to do and we're gonna go ahead and do it...

SANDY. I want you to let me take it from here.

> (*Beat.*)

JIM. I know this guy, okay? I've worked him all day. I got some particular insights into his inner workings, you know what I'm saying? The inner workings of his mind.

SANDY. I don't need to know about the inner workings of his mind, I just need to scare him into compliance.

JIM. Listen, I get it. I get what you gotta do and I got some experience with it myself. You and me, we're both gonna make really good cops one day, I can see that you've got a passion for law enforcement as well and...

SANDY. I was a cop for six years. Before that I was a Marine.

JIM. Cool. So this isn't like a stepping stone for you.

SANDY. Nope.

JIM. This *is* the stone.

SANDY. Yeah.

JIM. Cool. This bodyguard thing, it pays pretty good?

SANDY. I get by fine.

JIM. I'm asking cuz I'm thinking of taking a step up in my career, you know, maybe taking home a little more money at the end of the week.

SANDY. I don't want to drag this out any longer than it needs to be.

JIM. Alright. Alright.

> *(Beat.)*

But, just, you've got that cop intuition. When you look at me, you see a pretty strong guy right? I work out, you can see that.

SANDY. Okay.

JIM. So what does your training tell you about whether I'd be a good cop... You know, from your unique perspective.

SANDY. I don't have any idea...

JIM. I'm talking about intuition. Just you as a guy looking at me as a guy.

SANDY. I'm sure you'd be great at it.

JIM. That's good to know. Thank you. I may come a'calling on you, some point, some future point, recommendation letter maybe?

SANDY. If you don't mind, I'd like to get on with this.

JIM. Alright. Alright. I'll be right outside. Holding down the fort. If you need me. I'll just be holding down the fort.

> *(**JIM** reluctantly exits. **SANDY** goes to the bathroom, knocks, then opens the door.)*

SANDY. Come on out, please.

> *(**PETER** re-enters the hotel room, looks around, realizing **JIM** is gone.)*

PETER. Listen, sir, I'm sure you can see that man is deranged. He's unstable, he's harassing me, I've been held here against my will.

SANDY. I don't give a fucking shit about your will.

> (**PETER** *shuts up, suddenly scared.*)

This young woman that I'm protecting, she's important to me, okay? She's somebody I care about very deeply, beyond just the job. And if anything were to happen to her, anything physical or even if someone were to scare her, make her nervous, that would upset me. I would find that sort of thing *very* upsetting.

PETER. Of course.

SANDY. I'm going to need you to shut up, Peter. If you don't mind.

PETER. Okay.

SANDY. Shut the fuck up, Peter.

> (**PETER** *shuts the fuck up.*)

Whatever sick fantasy you have, whatever warped world view you've created to make yourself feel important, there's a person on the other end of that. And to get to that person, you have to go through me. I thought this was settled, but here you are again and I'm losing my patience. Are you going to make me hurt you Peter? No one would blame me. You're just some crazy fuck who wants to be close to something special. I'd be doing the world a favor.

> (**PETER** *stares at his feet. Terrified.*)
>
> (*And yet, there is something stirring within him.*)
>
> (*He looks up at* **SANDY**. *Stares him directly in the eye.*)

PETER. Go ahead and do it.

SANDY. Excuse me?

PETER. You heard me.

> (**SANDY** *looks at* **PETER** *for a moment, unsettled.*)
>
> (*There is a knock on the door.*)

JIM. (*Offstage.*) Sanford?

SANDY. Give us a minute.

(The knock comes again.)

JIM. *(Offstage.)* Sanford?

  *(**JIM** enters.)*

SANDY. What?

JIM. The, uh, your, um, your employer is here?

  *(**SANDY** looks at him, confused. **CHIARA** strides into the room. **JIM** follows her. **PETER**'s eyes go wide.)*

SANDY. Chiara, go back to the room.

CHIARA. *(Ignoring **SANDY**.)* Hi, are you Peter?

  *(**PETER** stares at her, dumbfounded.)*

Have they been terrible to you?

SANDY. Can I speak to you in the hall please?

CHIARA. Don't touch me.

  *(To **PETER**.)*

I'd like to speak to you in my room.

  *(**PETER** looks at her, stricken – "me?")*

SANDY. That's absolutely not going to happen.

CHIARA. You're fired, Sandy.

JIM. Yikes.

SANDY. Chiara, your mother and I…

CHIARA. You are fired.

  *(**SANDY** looks at her, unsure how to proceed.)*

*(To **JIM**.)* You're in charge here?

JIM. Yes I am.

CHIARA. This man is coming with me. Right now.

  *(To **SANDY**.)*

Stay away from me.

  *(To **PETER**.)*

Peter? Shall we?

  (Lights.)

Scene Two

(**CHIARA** and **PETER** in Chiara's hotel room.)

CHIARA. Thanks for coming.

PETER. Are you sure this is okay? Your guy seemed –

CHIARA. He's not my guy.

PETER. You have a restraining order –

CHIARA. Yeah, sorry. I take it back.

PETER. I think you have to do that legally.

CHIARA. You're shaking.

PETER. I'm nervous.

(Beat.)

CHIARA. So you love the show.

PETER. I do. I love the show.

CHIARA. You know Tom Driver who plays Harper?

PETER. Of course.

CHIARA. He wears a fedora like a hundred percent of the time and he goes to Brazil during hiatus and eats leaves with some guy he calls a shaman. And Pam Hollins who plays Gray? She boned the executive producer, that's why she came back as Calypso after the ship crashed. That's just like, some insider knowledge. Don't tell anyone I told you.

PETER. I won't.

CHIARA. What's your favorite episode?

PETER. Oh, man, that's a hard one. "Reflections" maybe? Or "This Too Shall Pass."

CHIARA. I don't really know the titles.

PETER. That's the one where you kill Dimitri.

CHIARA. Oh yeah. That was a fun one. It was like three in the morning when we shot that scene. I was freezing and like all hopped up on Red Bulls. My heart was pounding outta my chest. I was on this crazy diet where like, I could only eat organic kale, lentils, and Red Bull.

PETER. That doesn't seem healthy.

CHIARA. It wasn't supposed to be healthy.

PETER. What's your favorite episode?

CHIARA. I don't really watch the show. I liked the one where I got to wear that golden bone dress…

PETER. "Hexagon."

CHIARA. Sure.

    (Beat.)

You want something to drink?

PETER. What?

CHIARA. Like booze? You want booze? I got a minibar.

PETER. Oh, no. Uh, no thank you.

CHIARA. Oh. Is that weird? I felt like I should offer you something. Like, this is my home, basically. Like, welcome to my home. You're not gonna kill me are you?

PETER. No. No…

CHIARA. It would be super embarrassing if I came and bailed you out and then you killed me.

PETER. I promise I won't kill you. Or, or, anything. I won't do anything to you… I'm just, I wanted to meet you.

CHIARA. My mom's a bitch, okay? She's protecting her investment. One time I heard her call me a cash cow. I was seven. We used to live in Washington, back when my dad lived with us. We lived on a lake. I used to play with sticks and shit. I booked a commercial, so my mom moved us into a studio in Hollywood. We lived next to a hooker.

PETER. Where's your dad now?

CHIARA. Hong Kong. Well, the last time I talked to him Hong Kong, but that was a couple years ago.

    (Beat.)

I'm not trying to make you feel bad for me. My life is great, obviously, I know that.

(Beat.)

CHIARA. Do you have kids?

PETER. Two.

CHIARA. Should I sign something for them?

PETER. Oh. Sure. Thank you.

(An awkward pause.)

CHIARA. What should I sign?

PETER. Oh. I don't have anything.

CHIARA. Do you have like a phone or…

PETER. Oh. Yeah. Of course.

> (**PETER** *pulls his phone out of his pocket.* **CHIARA** *grabs it and then poses next to* **PETER**, *holding the phone out in front of her – taking a duck-faced selfie.)*

CHIARA. There you go.

PETER. Thanks.

CHIARA. What do your kids do? Like for fun.

PETER. William plays baseball. And Rayna's in the Girl Scouts.

CHIARA. I did Girl Scouts when we lived in Washington, but I had to stop when we moved. They don't have Girl Scouts in California.

PETER. I think they do.

CHIARA. No, my mom told me they couldn't get enough troops together.

> *(Realizing.)*

That's a lie, isn't it?

> (**PETER** *doesn't know how to respond. He waits.)*

So am I your favorite character on the show?

PETER. Yes. Definitely.

CHIARA. Why?

PETER. You're so strong. And you're young, but you see things so clearly. I think it's because you never knew what it was like on Earth before and so you have this strong sense of what's right and... I liked when you stood up for Gregor. When you pulled the drones off him and you almost died but you were willing to because he meant something to you...and I liked when he sacrificed himself because they were going to execute you...

CHIARA. That's why you're dressed as him. It's a good costume.

PETER. Thank you.

CHIARA. You identify with him or...

PETER. Well, he's one of the Indeterminants. And I've always sort of felt outside of things.

CHIARA. People say that a lot. Fans. I think everybody feels that.

PETER. Not everybody.

CHIARA. But like, everybody wants to be inside of something that they don't get to be. That's kind of the way life works, right?

PETER. For some people. Not for everyone. Some people get what they want.

CHIARA. Like who?

(Beat.)

Sabrina's probably the most badass character I've played. I have a trainer, this guy Brett. He was a Navy SEAL or something, now he wants to be an actor. But he sucks, and he has weird teeth. So like, "Not happening, Brett." He's a good trainer though. He's really into muscle confusion. You know about muscle confusion?

PETER. Not really.

CHIARA. Well it sucks but it's amazing. And I have to eat lean proteins all the time, then there's one day a week where I have to eat a bunch of fats. Like all the fat I can eat. It's weird. But it works. It's like, if you don't question everything all the time, you see results.

PETER. Well, you are beautiful.

CHIARA. You think so?

PETER. Everyone thinks so.

CHIARA. You know, I've never even had a boyfriend.

PETER. That can't be true. What about…

CHIARA. Jayden Church? Yeah, I mean, we've been seen together or whatever but most of that's for press 'cause I'm trying to transition to adult roles and he's trying to get more famous. My manager set it up. I don't know, the whole thing is fucked because like, I actually liked him. Like I'm stupid enough to be like, "Yeah, okay it's a fucking set-up, but he's actually kind of cute and what's so terrible about me that I shouldn't have a boyfriend?"

PETER. You're more talented than he is.

CHIARA. I know.

PETER. He's not even in your league.

CHIARA. I know. But at the same time, he's boning Jessa Andrews and I'm a twenty-three-year-old virgin.

> (*Beat.*)

Don't tell anybody that.

PETER. I won't.

CHIARA. Peter, I'm serious. Don't fucking tell anybody that.

PETER. I won't.

CHIARA. I'm not like, weird, okay? I've done plenty of other stuff, okay?

PETER. Okay.

CHIARA. I mean, fundamentally, we're all alone, right? It's so much effort keeping people interested in you. I'm practically throwing myself at Jayden and I don't think I'm bad-looking, like I'm not a bad-looking girl, I'm not an ugly girl.

PETER. You're the most beautiful thing I've ever seen.

CHIARA. Thank you.

> (*Beat.*)

You said thing.

PETER. What?

CHIARA. You said I'm the most beautiful *thing* you've ever seen.

PETER. I didn't mean… You're the most beautiful woman, person, human, but you're also, I mean, I've seen the Northern Lights, you're more beautiful.

CHIARA. What's that?

PETER. The Northern Lights?

CHIARA. Is that a band?

PETER. No. No, it's a phenomenon. Caused by energetic particles in the atmosphere. The whole sky lights up like a laser show. I used to see it when I lived in Alaska. You can't even believe what you're seeing. You've never seen pictures or anything? In a textbook?

CHIARA. Ha. Where would I get a textbook? I've been everywhere but I've never really been anywhere, you know?

PETER. Throughout history, people thought the lights were a sign from the gods, or ancient spirits dancing. But it's really science. You should make it a point to see it.

CHIARA. I've seen a lot of clubs, I guess. My mom likes to go to clubs all over the world. She grew up in Nebraska, they don't have a lot of clubs there. They've got like a lot of Arby's. We've gone to all the best clubs in Paris, in Milan, Vienna, we went to this one place in Zurich – everyone looked like they were wearing ski pants. You could hear their plastic pants rubbing together when they danced.

PETER. You never went camping or anything with your dad?

CHIARA. My dad was too busy fucking his assistant pharmacist to take me camping. Now he's married to her. I call her Pharma-tits.

> (*Beat.*)

Wanna see something amazing right now?

PETER. What is it?

CHIARA. It's a surprise. Wait there.

(*CHIARA stands up, grabs a duffle bag and runs into the bathroom.* **PETER** *waits. He takes in the room. Walks toward the bed. Then, thinks better of it. He walks over to the bathroom door. Listens.*)

(*Beat. Beat.*)

PETER. Are you okay?

CHIARA. (*Offstage.*) One second!

(**PETER** *sits. Readjusts. Stands. Then sits again.*)

(*There is a loud knock at the door.*)

(**PETER** *looks to the bathroom door.*)

(*The knocking continues.*)

PETER. Um…

CRYSTAL. (*Offstage.*) CHIARA!! YOU OPEN THIS DOOR RIGHT NOW!! RIGHT NOW!!

(**CHIARA** *re-emerges from the bathroom wearing a bathrobe with something unseen underneath.*)

(**CHIARA** *rushes to the door and locks the chain just as* **CRYSTAL** *gets the electronic key card to open the door. She pushes her face into the four-inch space made by the chain.*)

Chiara, open this door.

CHIARA. Leave me alone.

CRYSTAL. Open the door.

CHIARA. No.

CRYSTAL. Sweetie, what are you doing? Is he in there?

CHIARA. His name is Peter.

CRYSTAL. He's dangerous, Chiara.

(**CHIARA** *turns to* **PETER**.)

CHIARA. Are you dangerous?

PETER. No.

CHIARA. He's not dangerous. Leave us alone.

CRYSTAL. I get it. You want to punish me. I'm sorry. I should have told you about Sandy.

CHIARA. Ugh, Mom, I don't give a shit about Sandy. Not everything is about you. Just get out of the way, I'm shutting this door now.

CRYSTAL. Sweetie, I'm gonna have to ask the hotel to cut this chain.

CHIARA. I'll call the magazines and tell them you went bananas and started breaking down doors. They'll haul your ass in for a 5150. How about that?

CRYSTAL. Chiara.

CHIARA. Mom, Peter and I are in love.

> (CHIARA *looks at* PETER, *motioning for him to play along.* PETER *looks at her, stunned.*)

Like we may run away together. Like I'm naked right now.

> (CHIARA *keeps gesturing at* PETER.)

CRYSTAL. That's not funny. Chiara that's not funny.

CHIARA. Oh my God, Peter, that feels AMAZING. OH MY GOD. OH MY GOD IS THAT YOUR TONGUE?!

> (CHIARA *motions for him to sit. He sits.*)

GET BACK MOM. GO AWAY.

> (CRYSTAL *recoils enough for* CHIARA *to slam the door.* CHIARA *turns back to* PETER.)

She's just throwing her enormous weight around. You know she used to be super fat? It was crazy. So...

> (CHIARA *drops the bathrobe. Underneath she is wearing a costume, a beautiful glittering warrior shield, ropes bound around her arms.*)

You like?

PETER. Holy shit.

CHIARA. I know, right? This is what I wore when I killed Dimitri.

PETER. I know.

CHIARA. They let me bring it to conventions.

(She lifts the sword high above his head.)

CHIARA. I could kill you with this. It's actually sharp. Not like deadly sharp, but sharp enough to hurt someone. And like, you could hit someone with it, knock 'em out. Cool huh?

> (**CHIARA** *tip-toes back toward the door and looks through the peephole.*)

Mom. I can see you.

CRYSTAL. *(Through the door.)* Honey please.

CHIARA. LEAVE ME ALONE!

> (**CHIARA** *watches through the peephole for a long beat.*)

She's gone.

(Beat.)

She's fucking my bodyguard, y'know.

PETER. Is that why you fired him?

CHIARA. Well and cuz he's not a good bodyguard. I mean, like, no offense, but I mean, like you're here right now and I have a restraining order…

PETER. I wasn't trying to… I…

CHIARA. Relax, Peter. Sandy's been my bodyguard since I was like twelve. He thinks I'm a baby. He treats me like I'm his kid or something, instead of his boss. And I'm not down with that.

> *(She looks through the peephole again.* **CRYSTAL** *is gone. This lands on her. She covers.)*

Can I see the ring?

PETER. Oh. Yes. Of course.

> (**PETER** *fishes the ring out of his pocket. He produces a gold wedding band on a chain. She looks at it, doesn't take it.*)

CHIARA. Pretty.

(Beat.)

When were you gonna do it?

> *(Beat.)*

I've done fifty-two episodes. I know what a ring means.

> (**PETER** *looks at her, dumbstruck. Finally:*)

PETER. Tonight.

CHIARA. That's fucked up, you know. That you were gonna put that on me.

PETER. That's not what I was trying to do.

CHIARA. The security guy's never seen the show?

PETER. He watches *The Voice*.

CHIARA. I love *The Voice*.

> *(Beat.)*

So he didn't know what it meant.

PETER. He thought I was trying to propose.

CHIARA. How were you gonna do it?

PETER. I have a bottle of pills.

CHIARA. What kind?

PETER. Anxiety.

CHIARA. Xanax? Klonopin? Ativan?

PETER. Lithium. And a bottle of Vicodin.

CHIARA. You need booze too. You have booze?

PETER. Yes.

CHIARA. I used to want to kill myself. Everyone at school hated me, I had ano-fur on my arms, I was hungry all the time, all my friends were fifty-year-old hairdressers. I guess I got over it.

> *(Beat.)*

Sometimes if you just think about how one day you'll be dead, it can make you feel better.

PETER. That wasn't really helping.

CHIARA. You should write a note. I don't even know you. I wouldn't know what to tell your family.

PETER. My family doesn't care.

CHIARA. Yeah, you say that, but families are weird that way. They can be super shitty when you're alive but they almost always care that you're dead.

    (Beat.)

They'll be angry with you.

PETER. I don't think so.

CHIARA. What'd you do?

PETER. I came here.

CHIARA. What?

PETER. My wife told me not to come last year, but I did. So she took the kids and moved to Florida.

CHIARA. You're not really helping your case by coming back this year.

PETER. There is no case. It's unfixable.

CHIARA. Don't you love them?

PETER. Of course.

CHIARA. You shouldn't leave them, Peter. My dad left with Pharma-tits and now we've got no relationship. Like none at all. The only time I hear from him is in the press. "Chiara's Father Wishes Her a Merry Christmas." Like, great headline, you guys, real quality journalism.

    (Beat.)

Your kids love you. They just do. They can't help it. I did a Lifetime movie where I played this abused kid, my dad hit me and my mom made me sleep in a closet, and then I go and live at this old lady's house for the summer, she used to be a nun or something, it doesn't matter, but anyway she runs this farm for abused animals and I become friends with this goat named Rudy. And we hang out like the whole movie, and I start to come out of my shell, and my bruises fade, and then Rudy dies and it's super sad and then I go back and live with my mom. Point is, even kids that get abused love their parents. It's science.

(**CHIARA** *walks over to* **PETER** *and hands him the sword. Ceremoniously.* **PETER** *looks at her, unsure what to make of what is happening. Then,* **CHIARA** *looks at him and becomes another person, a character – her character from* Odyssey, *Sabrina, a warrior. She looks at* **PETER**, *fully immersed in her character.* **PETER** *looks on, mesmerized.*)

(*As Sabrina.*) What did they do to you? Oh God. Gregor. You can't do this. I need you. We all need you.

(**PETER** *looks at her, realizing what's happening.*)

(*Now saying Gregor's line, prompting him.*)

"They need you more, Sabrina. Without you there's no hope…"

PETER. (*Saying it with her.*) …No hope.

(*Then.*)

…There's just darkness and time.

(*They're acting it out now.*)

CHIARA. (*As Sabrina.*) But who will steer the ship? I can't drive that thing.

PETER. (*As Gregor.*) I'll meet you on the other side.

CHIARA. (*As Sabrina.*) It could be years before I die.

PETER. (*As Gregor.*) But for me, it'll just be a moment. Just a blink and we'll be together again. Without our bodies. And so, forever.

CHIARA. (*As Sabrina.*) I'll go with you.

PETER. (*As Gregor.*) No.

CHIARA. (*As Sabrina.*) We'll go together.

PETER. (*As Gregor.*) You have to stay. For them. Without you, this world dies. You know that.

CHIARA. (*As Sabrina.*) Is this rock even worth fighting for?

PETER. (*As Gregor.*) Think of Arthur. Think of Sam and Vero. There are people here who need you.

(PETER tightens his grip on the sword, prepared for the battle ahead.)

PETER. *(As Gregor.)* It's not an ending. It's a chance to start over. When you die you don't disappear. You become more a part of everything.

(He holds up the ring.)

CHIARA. *(Sabrina, speaking Ork.)* Darek sala throke vasa.

PETER. *(Gregor, speaking Ork.)* Throke mova.

(PETER stares at her, totally immersed in the world of the show. CHIARA leans in and kisses him.)

(Beat. The spell is broken.)

(As himself.) You shouldn't have done that.

CHIARA. I thought you said I was beautiful.

PETER. You are…but you can't…that's not how it…

(Beat.)

CHIARA. The dialogue's pretty whack sometimes, right? "Is this rock even worth fighting for?" The writers really milk that shit.

(PETER looks at her.)

PETER. I should go.

CHIARA. No! Let's do another. Wanna do the crash?

(Starting the next scene.)

Wingspeed is decreasing. Gregor, pull the airlock, release the cargo. This bird's going down!

(She stops, looks at him.)

You came all this way to see me. You're disappointed.

PETER. Not at all.

CHIARA. I can see it.

PETER. That's not how Gregor dies…

(CHIARA looks at PETER, picks up the sword. A transformation is taking place. Her face turns cold.)

I'm sorry, I –

(She raises the sword toward him.)

(As Sabrina.) You think killing Gregor will quiet us? You think his death isn't meaningful? Dimitri, you betray the people, they won't forget.

PETER. *(Realizing she's making him the enemy.)* Please, don't…

CHIARA. *(As Sabrina.)* Are you afraid? You should be. When you look at me, do you see all of them? Do you hear all their voices?

PETER. Don't make me Dimitri.

(She walks toward him, shoves the sword into his hand. She pulls his arms, pointing the sword toward herself.)

CHIARA. *(As Sabrina.)* Use it. There will not be another chance.

(There is an urgent knock on the door.)

PETER. Please.

SANDY. *(Through the door.)* CHIARA! OPEN THIS DOOR!

JIM. *(Through the door.)* PETER? YOU LEAVE HER ALONE!

*(**CHIARA** kneels before **PETER**, shoving his arms holding the sword toward her chest.)*

CHIARA. *(As Sabrina.)* Kill me, you coward!

(Looking him right in the eye.)

Go ahead and do it.

*(The electronic key opens the door on the chain. **SANDY** cuts the chain. The door opens. **SANDY** and **JIM** rush in, followed by **CRYSTAL**.)*

*(**CHIARA** stays on her knees in front of **PETER**. The following is overlapping, chaotic.)*

SANDY.	**CRYSTAL.**
Get away from her!	Chiara! Chiara!

JIM. Peter!

(**SANDY** *tackles* **PETER**. **CRYSTAL** *rushes to* **CHIARA**.)

SANDY. Get up.

(**PETER** *stands*. **SANDY** *has him tight*.)

(**CHIARA** *tries to intervene. She grabs* **PETER**'s *hand. They hold each other's hands.* **CRYSTAL** *tries to pull her off.*)

CHIARA. It's not his fault! Don't touch him! Stop it! He didn't do anything. Peter!

CRYSTAL. Get him out of here.

(**PETER** *locks eyes with* **CHIARA**. *In spite of the chaos around them, they are only looking at each other. As* **JIM** *and* **SANDY** *pull him from the room,* **PETER** *tries to calm* **CHIARA**.)

SANDY. Let's go. Come on.

PETER. It's okay. It's okay. It's okay. It's okay. It's okay.

CHIARA. I'm sorry.

(**SANDY** *and* **JIM** *escort* **PETER** *out of the room*.)

CRYSTAL. What did he do to you? Did he touch you?

CHIARA. He didn't do anything…it's my fault, I made him…

CRYSTAL. Enough, Chiara.

CHIARA. Somebody has to help him. He's got kids.

CRYSTAL. I don't want to hear another word about it. Let's get you changed.

(**SANDY** *re-enters*.)

SANDY. The police are on their way.

CHIARA. What's gonna happen to him?

CRYSTAL. Jesus Christ, this is a nightmare. I'm shaking. Look at my hand.

SANDY. We'll take her down the back elevator.

CRYSTAL. I'll call Donna. We're not doing that fucking panel.

CHIARA. What's going to happen to him?

> (*They stop and look at her.*)

CRYSTAL. Who cares?

CHIARA. I do.

> (**SANDY** *can see that she really needs to know.*)

SANDY. They'll get him some help.

CHIARA. I don't believe you.

> (**SANDY** *rethinks this. Decides to treat her like an adult.*)

SANDY. He'll go to the police station. They'll charge him.

CHIARA. It wasn't his fault.

SANDY. If you still feel that way in a few weeks, you can say it in court.

CRYSTAL. Can we get out of here please?

CHIARA. Will the police call his family?

SANDY. Probably.

> (**CHIARA** *takes this in.*)

CHIARA. You promise?

SANDY. He'll have to call someone.

CHIARA. Promise they'll call his family.

SANDY. It's up to him who he calls.

> (**CHIARA** *takes this in as* **SANDY** *turns to* **CRYSTAL**.)

Can you get her packed?

CRYSTAL. Yeah. Give me ten minutes.

CHIARA. How come we never went camping?

CRYSTAL. What?

SANDY. I'm gonna go check on the car.

CRYSTAL. No, Sandy, come on, she's just being funny, let's just all get out of here.

CHIARA. What Mom? You're scared to be alone with me?

CRYSTAL. What? Of course not. What are you talking about?

SANDY. I'll be back okay?

> (**SANDY** *slips out the door.*)

CRYSTAL. We'll have to give him a raise. You can't just go around firing people.

> (**CRYSTAL** *throws heaps of clothes into a suitcase, packing quickly.* **CHIARA** *stares at her mother.*)

CHIARA. I didn't ask for this.

CRYSTAL. Of course not, baby. That man was crazy.

CHIARA. He isn't crazy. That's not what I meant.

CRYSTAL. Go get your makeup. Come on, chop chop.

CHIARA. I'm not going with you.

> (*Pause.*)

CRYSTAL. This is about camping? You're mad I never took you camping. We went to Prague for Christ's sake. I didn't think you were the camping type.

CHIARA. We lived on a lake. We should have gone camping.

CRYSTAL. Well, I'm sorry. We can go camping. How about that? Now can you get your stuff together?

CHIARA. I'm not going, Mom. I'm going somewhere else. Maybe Alaska.

CRYSTAL. Oh yeah? Alaska? What's in Alaska?

CHIARA. The Northern Lights.

CRYSTAL. Great. Perfect. Go see the Northern Lights, get eaten by a bear.

CHIARA. Don't you ever miss the lake?

CRYSTAL. Um, no.

CHIARA. Never? You don't miss Dad?

CRYSTAL. Absolutely not.

CHIARA. You used to love him.

CRYSTAL. I used to weigh almost two hundred pounds too, you don't see me getting nostalgic about that "used to."

CHIARA. Mom.

CRYSTAL. What, Chiara? What do you want?

CHIARA. I want you to let me go.

CRYSTAL. I'm not your zookeeper. You're a grown woman. Go wherever you want.

CHIARA. I want you to be happy for me.

CRYSTAL. What should I be happy about? You know what's going to happen when you don't show up Monday morning? Well, first of all, Ron's going to be pissed, they'll write you off the show, ever thought of that? They wrote Jamie off, think they won't write you off? And then what…then you're in the magazines because you're being treated for "exhaustion"? Are you kidding? Every director's going to think you're a liability, that you're on meth or something, that you think you're some kind of diva, you don't show up for work. And you'll come to me mad in a year when you aren't working and say it was my fault for letting you do this. No, I'm sorry, but I'm not going to be happy for you to throw your life away so you can go to Alaska. I'm sorry but not happening.

CHIARA. I feel like we're moving around so much because we're afraid to look at each other. Like if we stop moving we won't be able to breathe. I don't know how to be a person. I've never even tried.

CRYSTAL. Sweetie, at some point, you grow up. People go to work. And this is what you do. This is your job.

CHIARA. But I just keep thinking, one of these days, my life will start. It'll really start.

(Beat.)

CRYSTAL. You know, your father was screwing around on me before we ever moved to LA. You should know that. He started screwing around on me six months after we got married.

(Beat.)

It's not like I took you away from a perfect life. That's all I'm saying. You can want to go camping and you can wish your dad was different, and you can wish I was different. But I did my best for you. And for me too. I did my best for both of us.

CHIARA. I know.

CRYSTAL. Don't go thinking I'm some kind of monster.

CHIARA. I don't.

CRYSTAL. I just tried to make all your dreams come true.

    (Beat.)

My dreams, maybe. I don't know. Who knows what a seven-year-old dreams about. But I remember you crawling into my bed in the middle of the night and whispering to me about how you were gonna be a star. You said that, not me. You were the one who said that.

    (Beat.)

You don't want to do this anymore? Let's not do it.

CHIARA. What would we do?

    (Beat. They look at each other for a long moment. Then, CRYSTAL *grabs the bags.)*

CRYSTAL. I'll be in the car.

    *(*CRYSTAL *exits.* CHIARA *watches her go. She stares at the door for a long moment. Then looks to the window.)*

    (Her eyes fall on PETER*'s ring on the floor. She goes to it, picks it up, looks at it. She closes her hand around it.)*

    (She turns. Walks to the door, opens it, and exits.)

End of Play

www.ingramcontent.com/pod-product-compliance
Lightning Source LLC
Chambersburg PA
CBHW070646120726
47909CB00004B/1597